BAD OLD BOY

MYRON SHERMAN

Primal Publishing · Allston, Massachusetts

© 2026 Myron Sherman

Book design by Michael McInnis
Cover illustration used with permission.

All rights reserved. This book or any portion thereof may not be reproduced or used in any manner whatsoever without the express written permission of the publisher except for the use of brief quotations in a book review or scholarly journal.

ISBN 978-1-971785-01-1

Primal Publishing
POBox 1179
Allston, MA 02134

For H.A.S.

Number A 3

Bad Old Boy 21

NUMBER A

THIS WAS NOT

your mother's Wetonawanda. Drag Hill sat looming over the Blackbird county seat like a pile of horseshit over another smaller pile of horseshit, and Johnny Piper sat in his rusted 1986 Dodge Dart in a copse of trees just off the road, waiting. Sometimes for the end of his self-appointed shift, so he could get home to his Plott hound Willie, sometimes simply for a kind word from his wife Dora. He didn't care that she'd been named for some famous long-dead woman the way she reminded him a couple times a week as he tried to make it with her in bed: he wanted maybe a kiss on the cheek. Romance. He wasn't a fucking machine. And she wanted Brady Bragg, drug dealer, twice-jailed hellion and raconteur.

Three weeks before, word had come down from above, the way it does, that his services were no longer required at one of his three jobs: the lightest job among them, cashier for the Dandy-Mart. With the news, Dora had packed two suitcases and her birth control pills, then hightailed it for the woods, without even a word of explanation. Her mobile phone number changed, he had no way of knowing exactly where she was, and he became, as his therapist would say, troubled.

He'd missed work, and work had missed him enough to reprimand him. Once. Then one incident at home piled over another like petty larcenies. Their daughter Sylvia, thirteen years old and already bitter like asparagus on the tongue, might be described one way as rebellious and another way as troubled as he was. His second job, at a night-shift-only adult bookstore called Frank's Films, fired him for conduct unbecoming a retail slut. Johnny realized now that nobody knew who Frank was, but it didn't matter, just like the methhead kids he was waiting in the trees for now, didn't matter. Here, Johnny was a guy waiting for another guy – Brady Bragg – who would sell another guy drugs – meth or crack or, scary for these times, injectables like heroin – then, snorting and hopping, or cranked to the gills, Brady would drag-race his buyer down the hill and into the half-mile straight stretch before the highway and the roadside bar and restaurant, Wheaty's. Winner got a free hit, and everybody left happy, scratching themselves bloody.

Today, though, Johnny had a radar gun and a .357 Magnum (these kids could get edgy) for backup. He reported the names of the buyers he saw to State

Police Officer Fritz, barracks conveniently located across from job number three, where Johnny janitored under contract via union to clean the rooms where his now-missing social worker wife saved marriages and counselled low-lives. It had been a hard but decent life, and now it was fucked. He heard the brassy gunpowder-like sound of Brady's glasspaks coming up the other side of the hill. Brady loved the car like a pet wolf, although he also loved beating it up on dirt roads and gravelly switchbacks all over the surrounding county. Brady's love had limits, in other words, which Johnny swore deep in his heart had something to do with Dora. He knew Dora was with Brady. No limits.

Soon Brady's Frankenstein monster Mustang came tearing down the road, a lean Trans Am not far behind, like it was 1985 again, a crescendo of exhaust fumes and whining engines passing quickly as a John Elway rifle shot from the pocket. Johnny hit the button on the radar gun to see 92 on the screen. He wrote down Brady's name, put a checkmark by it, and stowed the radar gun under the seat, shoving aside a tire tool kept alongside the shifter. He looked both ways before pulling off the service road and heading toward the racers. They'd already be in the bar, and tonight he didn't feel like following them in. It would have been better if he could represent himself as a regular. No such luck. He was not a bar drinker, Johnny was a home drinker. Fuck it, he decided. One drink, and he would see Brady's face at least, and know if Dora was with him.

Inside Wheaty's the lights were low and the noise came at Johnny like a wave. A DJ high on a rickety stage spun some remixed tune with a high synthesizer part that immediately grated. As with IHOP, cafeterias and most country bars, the 80s had never ended, but instead percolated softly in every person above a certain age, a certain swagger. Memories of the salad days. Brady and Beanie, a couple guys with full-sleeve tattoos and backward straight-brimmed hats took up two of the small tables. Brady nodded shortly in Johnny's direction. That's as much as I need, Johnny thought. He picked up his Budweiser and approached the table. Brady's right eyebrow was pierced and he had an ugly green neck tattoo.

"What up homes?" Johnny said.

Brady tipped a bottle in his direction. "You know, this and that, a bit of the other. You know." Their eyes locked for just a moment, cracked and tinted mirrors.

"I heard your car from way outside town just now. Loud as a motherfucker," Johnny said. "Real real loud."

"These kids all wanna make the noise," Brady said, "but they ain't got the shutup or the putup." He pointed with his bottle at Beanie, who had disappeared to the bathroom for a bump. "How you with putup, John?

"You know me. I do all right." Johnny said.

"I see you downtown pretty regular. Like Dora says, you got a habit of coffee at Molly's?" Molly's was a tiny cafe on the same street as the police station. It had never been robbed by Brady or his type due to the regular state police presence.

"I drink good coffee, man. Wherever I find it." A look at his watch convinced him he needed to exit soon, before he accidentally said the right thing. Brady had mentioned Dora, which should have sent him into Zone Violence, but something stopped him. Did Brady know his secret impotence? Had Dora told him?

"You one of those lazy-ass sons of bitches want a Starbucks on every corner. Vente motherfuckers got no sense. They need to keep out of shit, stick to the big cities. Elmira. Syracuse. Harrisburg," Beanie said, overhearing as he came banging through the restroom doors rotating his head back and forth. He looked at Johnny with undisguised contempt. "Who's the bitch?" Beanie said, sneering. Before Brady could answer, Johnny abandoned his already-tense acting and stepped into Beanie's chest, who pushed him back roughly. "Oh, you're a tough guy. 300 pounds of shit I be kicking down the river," Beanie said.

"Fuck off," said Johnny, pushing back. Brady stepped between Beanie and Johnny before it could go any further.

"Two assholes," Brady said. "Every stupid man ends up in monkey mind, like he ain't got sense." Brady rubbed his chin.

"The fuck, Brady?" Beanie said.

"It's a Zen thing. You're trying to calm your center and here comes a dude in monkey mind, got all sorts of stuff in his brain, dunno whether to shit or go blind. You got to chill, Beanie." Brady pushed Beanie and Johnny back, one hand each on their shoulders.

"And this fuck?" Beanie said, stepping back. "This your woman's man."

Brady held his breath for a moment, then blew it out. "He ain't nothing to stew about, Beanie. Check yourself. And Johnny. She ain't my woman. I'm just helping her."

"I was just leaving," Johnny said, shooting his cuffs as if he wore a suit. It was better to go when no one's pride had gotten too chippy. He'd have to be more careful next time. And there would be a next time. "Gentlemen," he said, and left his half-full bottle on Brady's table. Outside the darkness grew, and so did his anger.

. . .

Johnny drove home with one hand on the wheel and the other clamped on a whisky bottle he'd brought from under the seat between his legs. At every stop sign he'd take a pull, and in the 45 minutes it took him to get home, he'd gotten pretty well toasted. All the lights were off in their modular home except the one in Sylvia's room. Willie looked like he'd trampled Dora's flowers, all dirty nose and energy.

Once inside, he yelled to Sylvia. "I'm home." Sylvia came out from her bedroom, a petite girl with hair just beginning to show roots from the black dye she normally put in it. She snapped on the light as Johnny sat down heavily, whisky slopping on the sofa.

"You seen Mom?" Sylvia said. She crossed her arms.

"Nope. She's with Brady now. I don't know when or if we'll see her." He took a pull from the bottle. "You eat yet?"

"I already had a bowl of cereal. I didn't know when you'd be home."

"Give me a minute," Brady said, squeezing the bridge of his nose. "I'll boil some hot dogs and pierogies. You need more than cereal."

"It's fine, Dad. I'm fine." A long moment passed between them, during which Johnny took another sip. Just like that, he'd gotten drunk. "Aren't you going to go get her?" Sylvia said.

"It's not that easy if she doesn't want to come," Johnny said. He stood up and weaved toward the kitchen.

"But why?" Sylvia said. "What does Brady have that you don't? I mean, I'm here too. Does she not want to see me?"

"She'll be home to see you. Right now, she can only see Brady. And what he has, darlin', is dispensable income."

"You mean disposable income?"

"Exactly." He opened the bag of pierogies and dumped it into a pot, ran water over the top.

"You're supposed to boil the water first," Sylvia said.

"This way works too," Johnny said. He put a coffee cup under the Keurig and threw in a pod of Dunkin'. Then the button wouldn't work. He sighed.

"So what are you going to do?" Sylvia sat down at the kitchen table and worried at a strand of hair. She needed a trim.

"I already did it. Went to see Brady Bragg at the bar."

"Did you beat him up?"

"No." Johnny sat down at the table across from Sylvia and laced his fingers behind his head, trying to force his mind steadier.

"Why not?"

"A lot of reasons, some of them good. If he kicks my ass, who's going to take care of you now that your mother's gone?"

"Good point. I still wish you'd tried though." Sylvia got up and stirred at the pierogies with a wooden spoon.

"Wish I'd tried too," Johnny said. "Wasn't the right time."

"So you're going to get him?" She turned to face him.

"In my own way, yep." Johnny stood up, weaving a little. "Those done yet?"

Sylvia dug the sour cream out of the refrigerator and put some pierogies in a bowl for each of them, with a heavy dollop on top. They ate in silence, listening to the wind in the branches outside the screened kitchen window. In the distance Johnny imagined he heard the roar of glasspaks and saw in his mind Brady Bragg laid out on the hood of his fancy Mustang like a gutted deer. The thought gave him passing satisfaction.

• • •

Johnny woke five hours after he'd gone to sleep, ready to get to his job cleaning the strip mall offices of Kings Realty, Wetonawanda Savings and Trust, and most importantly, New Wings Psychotherapy, the place Dora worked. He'd managed to make it to work these past three weeks, but she hadn't, taking a month off, according to her supervisor, under the Family and Medical Leave Act. Which left her a week to get her shit together, not that he was going to wait that long for her to make a decision between him and Brady Bragg. Needless to say, he didn't believe Brady. They were together. Johnny showered under a roaring head of steam, shaved and laid out a banana and a packet of Quaker Oats for Sylvia when she awoke.

The Dart started with a roar – good bones, that car had, but a Bondo body – and he pulled out of the pitted dirt driveway for the trip into town. When he got in, he pulled a ring of keys off his belt and opened the utility office, pushed the cleaning cart down the strip.. Kings Realty didn't take long; he only had to pop the trash bags off their cans and vacuum the rugs, wipe down the phones and the glass front door. The Savings and Trust took somewhat longer. He needed a key and a key card both. The electronic front door locks and the loss prevention system didn't work together, and more often than occasionally he'd have to call and wake the grumbling manager to come down and reset the alarm before the state police showed up, guns drawn. Today, luckily, was not one of those days, though some fucking joker had left two leaky garbaged bags on the floor that he had to haul out the back door and down the short hallway to the Dumpster, then scrub the carpets.

This left New Wings. He squeegeed the front window and door first, then opened the lock and emptied the recycling and refilled the tissue boxes in each separately locked and keyed door, squirted sweet-smelling sanitizer in the bathroom pot and swirled it around with the toilet brush. Dora's office door had a poster of an Amazon rainforest. Inside, it smelled like chrysanthemums, and glossy photos of Sylvia covered a corkboard over her desk. Hang in there, a cute little monkey said, dropping by a red ribbon from the side of her ancient computer. He sighed and looked around. For a sentimental woman, she didn't show it when he came into the picture, or more accurately, the lack of pictures. He couldn't see any reflection of himself anywhere in Dora's office except in the trash he emptied and the community refrigerator he cleaned. He traced her desk blotter and came to the five days a month she affixed with a red X to denote her period. There weren't any marks for the last month. A penciled line offset the margin with two phone numbers. Johnny pulled out his phone and entered both of them as Numbers A and B. He supposed that was something she must have considered before she'd FMLA'd with

Brady Bragg. He locked the doors behind him.

Outside, under the overhang, he hauled a hand truck filled with six flats of soda and water. He keyed open the two soda machines at once – no one here to complain at this hour – and begin filling the slots two cans at a time until he'd finished. Finally, he'd swept the concrete frontage and emptied the two huge trash receptacles at either end and the smaller one at the sidewalk entrance. By then Betty from the bank had pulled into the back, waved to Johnny, and walked around to the front to let herself in. Johnny had finished for the morning. He pulled a warm soda from the flats stored in the utility office and sat on the concrete. It was time for his unofficial government job, watching for speeders and looking for Brady Bragg and the other small-time dealers to make a mistake.

. . .

State Trooper Arnold Fritz had clued him in to this job one night after he'd come in to rent Hookers and Blow for the third time in a month. Johnny handed him a ten and a five back from his twenty--nobody worried about change – and they'd gotten to talking, no one else in the place.

"Got a job for a guy who can keep his mouth shut," Fritz had said, toothpick hanging out of his mouth, moving up and down against his yellow teeth as he sucked at it. "Pays 20 bucks an hour, maybe 20 hours a week, varying hours. In fact, once you learn the job, you could pretty much call it any way you see fit." Johnny thought of the extra money he could make in his off hours.

"I'm listening," Johnny had said. Fritz sat with him a few times to teach him the ropes, and it wasn't as if Johnny didn't know the criminals in town already."All right," Johnny had said to himself. "All right." And so it was. In no time he was sitting on service roads and in certain alleys, visiting the truck stop on 14 and the other adult bookstore, making note of who broke the limit and who sold the speed, all so Fritz could come in when the criminals got lazy and make the bust that would satisfy his superiors and kick him up the line into a cushier job and a better assignment. No one wanted to stay in Wetonawanda for very long.

. . .

Later that afternoon Johnny waited for Brady Bragg to come and make his daily run to Wheaty's. In the meantime, he kept alternating his thumb between Number A and Number B on his phone. Number B was a 607 area code, purchased somewhere in neighboring New York state, so he decided to try it first. He pushed the button and after a few moments a man picked up. "Brady," the man on the other end said. "Who's this?" Johnny groaned at the voice and thumbed it off. Fucking Brady.

Just in case push came to a motherfucking shove, Johnny had a five-gallon can of gas in the trunk and an old lockable Zippo lighter stashed in his pocket. Before he pushed Number A, he brought the Zippo out and set it on the seat next to him.

Johnny managed to clock the sixteen-year-old Vanderpool kid doing a smoking 110. He put a double check next to Vanderpool. The fourth time he'd noted him this month. He'd be off the road soon via Fritz or via accident. Around four in the afternoon, just as it started getting dark, Brady Bragg came roaring through at his usual 90 miles per. No one followed him today. Brady got out of the car in the Wheaty's parking lot, and he had a woman with him. And a girl. Sonofabitch. Dora. Johnny angrily pushed the button. A businesslike pleasant woman answered the line. "McKinley Fertility Center," she said. "How may I help you?"

"Can I speak with Dora Piper?" he said.

"You just missed Ms. Piper," the woman said. "Now what was your name again?" Johnny thumbed off the line and contemplated what he had learned.

The three of them disappeared into Wheaty's. Johnny guessed they were going to eat dinner. Brady had taken his wife, now he would take his daughter too? Not hardly. Brady walked down the road, gas can banging against his thigh, tire iron in his off hand. He took the half-mile of road as quickly as he could. Seven or eight cars and a couple trucks remained in the driveway with Brady's Mustang. He walked over quickly and smashed in the driver's side window of Brady's ride and opened up the car. It took only seconds to douse the leather interior. Johnny backed up and threw the lit Zippo into the car where it exploded into a tiny poof of flame that grew larger and larger by the moment. With it, Johnny felt his hopes for a happy family from these ashes grow modestly too.

When the car had taken off sufficiently, he walked inside, the tire iron still in his hand. Dora and Sylvia and Brady sat at a back table, eating cheeseburgers and fries. Nobody at the table looked comfortable, and it took Johnny only a sad moment to realize he'd irrevocably fucked it up.

"It's not what you think." Brady looked up at him, a weary look of resignation in his eyes, then at the tire iron. "But you know that don't you? What the fuck do you want then?" Brady said.

Johnny swallowed." Wanted to tell you," he said softly. "Your car is on fire." Just then an explosion shook the room to cries of astonishment and alarm from the patrons. Brady leapt up and rushed outside. Two of three people followed him excitedly.

"Johnny," Dora said, her eyes ufilling. "I wanted to have a baby. But you." She left the sentence un-finished. All around them the restaurant emptied. A swell of noise came through the door, and the smell of burning gas, an undertone of leather. The sound of sirens in the distance.

BAD OLD BOY

CRATE LANG

took a heavy blow against his chin, feeling the ring on Robbie Moore's finger crack against the dimple his wife loved, sending a dull ache into his entire jaw. Robbie pulled his fist back and circled around Crate like a boxer, hands up in front of his own face, glowering like a cartoon bulldog. Crate had a habit of fucking up.

"I told you," Robbie said. "You fuck with me, you pay." Crate crouched into his own stance and then thought better of it. What possible good could this do?

"Fuck it," Crate said, straightening. He offered his open hands to Robbie. "You're right. I fucked with the wrong man. You're a good ole boy, Robbie, and I don't want to fight you. Here –" Crate held up one hand, palm out, and reached for his wallet with the other. "I owe you a hundred bucks. Take one twenty five."

"It's worth three hundred," Robbie said uneasily. "My brother Dexter said you were a straight shooter."

"But we agreed on a hundred. I'm giving you a buck and a quarter." Crate held out his wallet and shook it.

"That pup is a gold mine," Robbie said.

"You didn't pay a red cent for that pup and it's never treed a coon," Crate said. "I'm giving you a deal. My kid needs a pup even if it won't tree."

"I still feel like you're ripping me off," Robbie said, and held out his hand. Crate counted out six twenties and five ones.

"And you got me one on the jaw," Crate said. "I'll forgive that little forget-me-not." All around them the crowd of men dispersed, murmuring. The small group of farmers and 4H leaders went back to the tractor pulls in front of the grandstand, and Crate sighed with relief. The pup was wormy and poor, but his grandsire had been a hell of a dog, and he hoped the blood would tell. And if it didn't, even then, little Jefferson would crow over it, and Jeanelle would have to make the best of it, as she so often did with Crate.

. . .

Crate drove his Ford Escort back over Chimney Hollow Road with the dog in the passenger seat, keeping between the ditches and swerving occasionally for potholes, the dust swirling up into his open window. He'd opened a bottle of water and left it in the cupholder, and already the mouth of it tasted like dirt.

Jeanelle would have dinner ready by now, and Jefferson would be sitting in his high chair with a plastic bowl full of Cheerios and his sippy cup. Crate sighed. He'd worked from four AM to four PM before stopping to see Robbie Moore about the dog. "Gonna call you Butch," Crate said, scratching the pup behind its ears. The pup licked his jowls. "I know. I'm hungry too."

The road bottomed out near a farm pond surrounded by white fence, a couple ducks swimming on its surface. Crate saw the trailer laid out on the other side of the road, skirting piled hip-high by the front door. He'd hoped to put it on this past weekend, but Jeanelle's mother Sarah and her boyfriend Cal showed up and five bottles of wine later he didn't feel like putting it up.

Jeanelle pitched a little fit about it, but smiled thinly as Sarah and Cal drove off, Jefferson squalling on her hip. She'd spoken to Crate only briefly since then, and he hoped to make it up to her with the pup, but he was half-certain she wouldn't believe he'd gotten the boy a coonhound, even though he'd extolled the virtues of boy and dog many times before.

Pulling into the front yard, he hit the brakes slightly

as he drove over the drainpipe and parked next to Jeanelle's truck. He gathered the pup in one hand and the worming medicine in the other and went into the trailer. The trailer smelled of fried chicken, and a slight mist gathered around the globe of light in the kitchen. Jeanelle had put on lipstick, which was unusual during the day, and she'd changed Jefferson into a clean onesie for dinner. The boy battered his cup against the plastic chair, chanting Da-DA, Da-DA, Da-DA, which made Crate feel pretty good, all things considered.

"Look what I got for you," Crate said, putting Butch up to the boy's face. Jefferson sniffed once and grabbed the dog by the ears. "Da-DA," he said.

"Yep, it's me. This here's Butch," Crate said. Jeanelle came around the table and touched the dog on the head.

"It's a nice dog," Jeanelle said. "I just wish you'd told me first." She took the dog down and drew some water in a margarine bowl and tucked it near the garbage can, where Butch began slopping it.

"I had an opportunity," Crate said. "I just couldn't pass it up."

"What happened to your face?" Jeanelle said.

"Nothing," Crate said. "Met up with a wrench. Bruised me a little."

"Uh-huh," Jeanelle said, her eyes half-lidded. "Dinner's on." Crate sat down at the table next to Jefferson and fed him applesauce from his own spoon. "So how was work?" Jeanelle kept asking him how work was going, but it didn't change much from day to day. Still new at the job, Crate spent a lot of days on top of a machine breaking rocks too large to go through the hopper, then at the end of the day helping the regular drivers grease the loaders and doing whatever else came up for the man on the lowest end of the seniority list.

"It was fine. Busted rocks, helped Ricky adjust the belts thirty feet up in the air." Crate pulled a piece of chicken out from his teeth.

"A little dangerous." Jeanelle toyed with the food on her plate. "I worry about you crawling around on top of the plant."

"No worries, babe," Crate said. "It's just that everybody has to do it. Eventually somebody else will be the low man and I'll be doing something else. The pay is great." He tried to change the subject. "How was your day?"

Jeanelle took a sip of her iced tea. "It's fine. Mom called. She and Cal picked up a new washing machine from the Deckers. It's mostly new. Sheila Decker just decided she wanted a new one so they sold it off for cheap."

"That's good," Crate said. "This chicken is fanfuckingtastic."

"Creighton. Why are we talking about the chicken?" Jeanelle folded her hands under her chin.

"What?"

"You didn't get that bruise from a wrench. I can see the mark of a knuckle or something."

"It's nothing, Jean. I had a disagreement with Robbie Moore, Dexter's brother. About the dog."

"So he hit you."

"He wanted more money than I was willing to pay."

"So he hit you?"

"I wanted the dog. We agreed on a price, then it wasn't what he wanted. I paid him a little more."

"How much more?" Jeanelle said.

"Just twenty-five bucks."

"How much did you pay for the dog?" Jeanelle sat back in her chair.

"Not much."

"We need that money," Jeanelle said. "The baby's doctor bill is due soon, and we haven't paid off my hysterectomy yet. I understand you wanted a dog for Jeff, but it's just not good right now."

"I'll get some money," Crate said. "Maybe I can pick up a little more overtime."

"You're working sixty hours a week already. You're going to fucking kill yourself." Jeanelle's eyes rose in tears.

"What choice do we have?" Crate said. "I just wanted a dog. The doctors can wait another month. Jeff's only going to be young once."

"He's only a little over a year old."

"It's important to start him out right. I didn't get a dog until I was five and I was already scared of them. I want Jeff to grow up with one, so he's not scared. I don't want him scared." Crate straightened his back and put his fork down. "I'm not hungry anymore."

"Crate. Don't do this."

"I've got a little daylight left. I'm going to hang that skirting around the front, so we don't look like white trash." Crate's chair banged back against the moulding as he rose. It was 6:30. He had maybe two or three hours of daylight left, and a load of anger with no place to put it.

. . .

Crate hauled a square of skirting up and leaned it against the trailer. He picked up a bottle of beer and drained half of it. Hipster beer, but he liked it. Fuck it. "Jeanelle," he called in through the screen door. "Get Jeff around. We're going to get ice cream." Inside the trailer he heard Jeanelle say something indistinct, and Jefferson's babbling reached a high pitch, then relaxed again like a bubble bursting. Ice cream would be a good thing, something to get his mind off his money trouble and onto something other than the troubled expression he'd seen on Jeanelle's face. It would take the last twenty dollars in his wallet, but it'd be good for everyone. Jeff would make a mess that Crate could clean up with baby wipes and get back on her good side, and later on in the dark while Jeff slept they could move together.

Jeanelle came to the door and poked her head out. "You're sure? Four is going to come awful early."

"I need to get out. You need to get out."

"I'm not going to lie. A hot fudge sundae would go down sweet." Jeanelle's head disappeared, and Crate picked up his T-shirt and put it back on, tucking the hammer and box of nails under the trailer. He stopped by the back of the trailer and washed his hands and face under the outside spigot. He considered his options. He could work overtime, provided the opportunity presented itself. He could cut wood on weekend nights and sell it this fall. He could get another job, but he needed something quicker than that, something that would quiet Jeanelle's worries and provide for Jefferson. He wondered if his mother-in-law's boyfriend needed any extra help. Cal installed security systems for the newly gas-rich farmers who suddenly had more money than they'd ever had before and wanted to protect their assets. Eventually that business would slow, but right now a lot of well-off farmers had bought expensive guns and entertainment systems, and needed protection from the itinerant gas industry workers who'd been shipped in from all over the country as well as the local tweakers. He could talk to Cal about that tomorrow after work.

Jeanelle came out with Jeff on one hip, locking the trailer door behind her. Crate jumped in on the passenger side of her truck, fastened Jeff into his car seat and the dog sat on the floor next to his feet. Jeanelle adjusted her side mirror and they left, bumping over the drainage ditch and down the dirt road to Coryland Road and eventually toward the Fair Shake. The country sat in full bloom around them, the fields heavy with hay and oats and the green trees beyond, still full of middle-growth trees and large patches of evergreen. Crate and Dexter had been out last week spotting deer and counted sixty-five before they got bored and started back for home. The black bears were out in abundance, and except for the frackers and the passingly curious fact that there were still very few jobs, the place was ideal for an outdoors-oriented family.

The blacktop road ran before them bright and shiny, one of the fringe benefits from the natural gas industry. All those trucks running back and forth needed good roads, and they roared down the hill at sixty-five miles an hour just because they could, singing along to country songs on the radio. They crossed into New

York and slowed the truck before turning left into Pine City. The Fair Shake did a banging business during the summer, even though the sundaes had gotten more expensive like everything else. People liked to sit at their picnic tables and eat their butter pecan ice cream in peace, gossiping with the neighbors they knew they'd find there.

Jeanelle walked up to the window with Crate's wallet in her hand and ordered while Crate and Jeff sat at a table and waited for her. She came back first with her sundae and Jeff's baby cone, then went back to pick up Crate's vanilla malt. Tonight they had the place nearly to themselves. Another couple and their small children gathered around the goldfish pond with their cones and a larger group had gathered near the rear, talking loudly and ordering multiple large sundaes to share. Soon he saw his good friend Dexter Moore pull up with his girlfriend Caitlin, and he left Jeanelle talking with a friend of her mother's and went over to talk with Dexter.

"Hey Dex," Crate said.

"I hear you tangled with Robbie today." Dexter Moore stood about six feet tall and maybe a hundred thirty pounds of wire and muscle in a green T-shirt. He worked for the cable company as an installer and always seemed to have a finger in money-making schemes. He'd never involved Crate, but Crate trusted him, and he thought quickly about his current situation and decided what the hell. He'd see what his friend had to offer.

"Wasn't much of a tangle. He got his money," Crate said, dangling his milkshake from one hand.

"Sorry about that. Robbie's a pushy sonofabitch." Caitlin sighed dramatically and left Dexter to go talk with Jeanelle.

"I know it now. Hey man," Crate lowered his voice so Jeanelle couldn't hear. "I need to make some quick cash. You know of anyone hiring or anything I could get into?"

"I don't know, man," Dexter said. "How bad off are you?"

"Oh you know. Bills and stuff. I just can't get ahead. I could use a couple extra checks."

"Couldn't we all?" Dexter said. " I don't know, man."

"Come on. You must know something. I know you're never hurting for money. You've always got extra."

"I can float you a couple hundred right now if you need it," Dexter said.

"Nope. I don't want to borrow. I want to make."

Dexter lowered his voice to a whisper. "If you can keep it quiet, I know a way you can make an easy grand. You have to come through though, because I'd be letting you in on it with these guys who don't like changes. I'm flush right now, but you can do the thing. It's basically just making a run into Syracuse and coming back. Easy-peasy. You show up, hand them the package, they hand you money. Cash and carry. Once every month. By December, all your money problems could be solved. It ain't exactly above board, though."

Crate thought of Jeanelle. Jefferson. More overtime. Never being able to get ahead. Just then the dog ran over to him, followed by Jefferson squealing and toddling his way over. "That's OK," Crate said. "I'm in."

. . .

Later that night, Jeanelle straddled him on the bed while Jefferson slept in the crib on the other side of the room. Crate was distracted and even though he performed all right his mind kept running off in different directions like a dog catching all the scents at once. Jeanelle finished but he didn't, and she tumbled off him in a heap and tucked herself into his arm. "Sorry baby," Crate said, cradling her breast in his hand.

"I'm sorry I got on you about the dog. It'll be a good thing." Jeanelle toyed with his chest hair.

"Yeah, Jeff sure likes him."

"Did you see the way he ran in the parking lot? Those little stumpy legs."

"Hey Jeanelle." Crate turned toward her. "I think I'm going to call Cal in the morning on the way to work, see if he has anything I can do on weekends. Get some money to get ahead a little."

"I don't know. Maybe that would work. He doesn't have anybody helping him any more, but he'll probably need more hours than you can give."

"Maybe this winter then. After I get laid off."

"It'd be nice not to have to rely on unemployment this winter." Jeff squalled a little in his sleep, and Jeanelle got out of bed to soothe him with a bottle.

"I got a feeling everything's going to work out,"

Crate said, even though he was unsure. Jeanelle needed to hear it.

. . .

The next morning on the way in to work Crate left a message on Cal's cell phone. Cal called him back on his way home.

"You need money, son?" Cal's voice was hard and angular in Crate's ear, but he knew he meant well.

"Everybody needs money, Cal."

"I don't have nothing for you on weekends. Most of my work is done in the week. Only once in a while these rich rednecks want me to come in and rewire their houses then. They want the weekends for fun."

"I thought it was worth the effort. Thanks Cal. How's Sarah?

"She's a mean old lady just like always." Cal laughed. Crate laughed back at him and pressed off the phone. He'd just turned on the radio when his phone buzzed again, this time with a text from Dexter: *they want the delivery tonight. u ready?*

Crate pulled the car off to the side of the road and

texted him back. The phone buzzed again almost immediately with an address near Syracuse: Lafayette NY. He'd have to fill the tank before he left. It was 4:15. He texted Jeanelle and told her he'd be home really late. He blamed it on Dexter needing help, as he sometimes did. Jeanelle wouldn't think it too much out of the ordinary. Crate felt a surge of adrenaline come over him. He drove to Dexter's house to pick up. Dexter waited outside, smoking a cigarette, a smaller package than Crate expected clutched tightly in his right hand.

"Hey man," Crate said. Dexter handed him the package.

"You ready for this?" Dexter said.

"Ready for what? Just a delivery. In and out. Like delivering a pizza." Crate knew it was more than that. He just didn't want to admit his nerves in front of Dexter. He'd given him an opportunity here, and he didn't want to fuck it up.

"Not exactly," Dexter said. "Just, you know, be cool. Jimmy is the guy you deliver to. Nobody else."

"Got it. Jimmy."

"All right man. Don't stop for anything between here and there. Too much risk."

"Dude. I got to get gas."

"If you have to," Dexter said.

"You said this was simple."

"Simple is as simple does." Dexter's throat flexed as if he was about to say something else.

"Are you fucking Forrest Gump?" Crate said.

"I'm beginning to regret this."

"Now, don't. I can do this."

"You better be able to. " Dexter thought for a moment. "Shit. I'll make the run with you."

"No need," Crate said. "I got this." Crate had second thoughts, honestly. Third thoughts, even. But now he had to go through with it. The thoughts of bills paid, a new coop for the dog, new brakes and tires on both vehicles. A nice place he could take Jeanelle to.

"All right. Here goes." Dexter tossed him the package. Stick it under your seat and go. Bring me back the money."

"I'm on it, Dex. And thanks."

"Don't thank me," Dexter said quickly.

. . .

Crate tucked the package under his seat. He figured it contained pills. He'd always known what Dex was into, so this came as no surprise, particularly the way things were these days. If it wasn't pills, it was meth, or something worse like heroin. Everybody had their crutch. Today people were more open about their pill addictions. Opioid epidemic my ass, Crate thought. What it is is a pain epidemic, and no way for most people to deal with it. He turned down the visor of his car and retrieved his sunglasses. It seemed hotter and brighter than ever.

He drove across the border into New York, trees surrounding him, an occasional gas truck rumbling by, but they were few and far between even now. The gas boom had come and gone, and people still clung to the idea of hitting it rich off their land even when the frackers had already gone in under the neighbors land and pulled it out anyway. No gas left, no industry left, pop. People like Dexter, who had been employed by Chesapeake, now had to sell pills to make money.

Crate took side streets whenever he could, trying to stay off the main road for fear of getting stopped. Most of the way involved route 81, so he couldn't really avoid cops. A trickle of sweat slid down his arm. Simple, he thought. Like delivering a pizza. He thought of Jeanelle. She'd like the money, but not the idea of him delivering pills. He'd have to keep the money safe somewhere and bleed it out over several weeks, so she wouldn't suspect something. He had to get on and help Cal or get a second job somewhere to justify the extra money. He'd end up having to work even harder to fake making money. Damn. He glanced at his phone. The GPS told him he had about twenty minutes before he came to the place where he was to meet Jimmy. Only Jimmy.

Crate pulled the Escort into a stripmall parking lot. The sun had about set, and shadows grew in the short pine trees growing in the mulched split between lots. He eased into a spot next to a 2018 Lexus in front of a tattoo parlor and a Granny's Pizza Palace. The address matched the pizza place. Unsure of what to do next, Crate sat there for a moment, then thrust his heel into the floorboards to put the package inside his pants, hanging his shirt over it. At the front window, he could see a man sitting, the only one in the pizza place. Fuck it.

He got up and went inside. The smell of dough and the sound of 80s music smacked him right in the face. Good smells, if not exactly comforting. "You know where I can find Jimmy?" he said.

The cashier looked him up and down. "Why? You looking for a job?"

"Yeah. He told me to show up. Tell him Dexter Moore sent me." Crate stuffed his hands inside his pockets. He'd expected something else. A house. An apartment building. Not a pizza place.

"Huh. Jimmy's next door. On his *lunch* break. Tell him we're getting busy over here." The man turned away, and Crate left.

The front door of the tattoo parlor hung heavy with a bead curtain on the inside that rattled when he opened it. Inside, the atmosphere was all metal and plastic, very uncomfortable, the kind of doctor-like atmosphere that gave Crate the nervous twitches. On a white table sat two thick books. One man waited, reading a magazine. Soon the tattoo artist came out. He stood easily a foot over Crate and maybe three hundred pounds, a tall thick giant, covered in ink except for his face and neck. "What can I do for ya?" the man said. "I'm Mack, the artist."

"I'm looking for Jimmy," Crate said. Mack looked him over carefully, eyes narrowed. He jerked his head toward the back.

"Jimmy's back there, in the break room." Crate wondered why the manager of the pizza place got to take his break in the tattoo parlor, but figured he wasn't getting paid to think. He was getting paid to deliver. Crate entered the back room just as a man exited the bathroom, zipping up. He too, was covered in tattoos, and wore the same red shirt the cashier in the pizza place wore.

"Who the fuck are you?" the man said.

"Dexter Moore sent me," Crate said. "You got somewhere we can talk?"

"Open your mouth," Jimmy said. "Or I'll stomp your ass."

"Back up," Crate said. "I got a delivery for you." He motioned to Jimmy. "You sure you want to do it here?"

"I don't know you or motherfuck anything," Jimmy said. "Get your ass out the door." Mack came back through the door.

"Keep it down. I got clients out here." Mack barely paid attention to Crate, his eyes flicking over him briefly as he addressed Jimmy.

"Come on out back," Jimmy said. he pointed to a steel door next to the bathroom. Crate took a deep breath and followed Jimmy outside. They paused beside a small Dumpster. Mack, behind Crate, suddenly clamped his arms behind him in a vise-like grip.

"The fuck?" Crate managed to say, just before Jimmy hit him in the gut, nearly doubling him over. Then the blows came hard and heavy to his chest and gut and arms, again and again.

"Hold him up, Mack," Jimmy said, as if from far away. Crate hung limp in the huge man's arms, He'd puked, and his chest felt as if it had been stomped by elephants. "I'd hit you right in your motherfucking stupid face if I didn't have to make pizzas all night," Jimmy said. Mack let Crate go and he tumbled to his knees, retching. Crate reached into his pants and felt Mack kick him in the stomach, and the package fell to the ground, where Jimmy picked it up. "You are a stupid motherfucker. Tell Dexter he needs to come himself next time, or we're going to have a bigger problem with him than we just demonstrated with you. Jam a 2x4 up his skinny ass and break it off."

Mack knelt down next to Crate, who gasped for breath, and put a hand on his back. "Stay down. You'll be fine in a few minutes. Then get out of here."

The entire thing took maybe ten minutes. Crate collapsed into a ball and passed out.

. . .

The strip-mall lights kicked on at nine PM, and Crate woke up. It had been nearly an hour since he'd had the piss beaten out of him by Jimmy and Mack, and walking around the front, he could see the tattoo place was closed, but the pizza place did a roaring business. Six or seven cars parked in the lot, a whole crowd of people in the place. he couldn't start something even if he'd been capable. Twice in two days people had hit him. There would not be a third time. Crate took stock of himself. A rib twinged, and his chest felt like someone had hollowed him out from the inside. They'd left his face alone, but he'd be feeling the effects of this for days, if not weeks. And he had to come home to Jeanelle and Jefferson. And he'd have to explain to Dexter why he didn't have any money for the pills. He unlocked his Escort and felt under the seat. For some reason his jaw ached. All those body shots. What the hell would he say to Jeanelle? As if on cue, his phone vibrated, and he ignored it.

He took the drive back slowly, listening to the 80s station on the radio. He had no reason to worry about getting stopped at 9:30 at night, but he looked at every exit for a cop anyway, force of habit. He stopped in Elmira at a 7-11 for a six-pack of beer, texting Jeanelle at the same time, but didn't crack one until he sat in his driveway, car engine ticking. Outside the house, the door light kicked on, and he took half a beer down in one swallow and sighed. He closed the door behind him softly, as Jefferson lay sleeping in his swing. Jeanelle sat in the chair, arms crossed.

"So?" Jeanelle said softly. He steeled himself. She was such a good woman, and he'd fucked up.

"Dexter gave me some stuff to deliver up to Syracuse. Some guys. They took a disliking to me, and I couldn't tell them what they wanted to hear, so they tuned me up a little."

"Tuned you up." Jeanelle got up and crossed the carpet, touching his shoulders. "Are you hurt bad?"

"They pretty much stayed in the body," Crate said, wincing as her hands traced his ribs.

"You're red," she said. "You're going to bruise up pretty bad. Are you going to work?"

"I don't have much choice, do I?"

"Does Dexter know?" Jeanelle's voice had taken an edge.

"Not yet. I should probably drive over there."

"You don't have what he needs." It wasn't a question, but he answered it anyway.

"No," Crate said. "I don't."

"How much money?" Jeanelle said.

"I don't know. They were supposed to give me an envelope to bring back."

"Oh Crate." She took his hand. "Deal with it tomorrow."

"I better do it tonight," Crate said. "Bad news doesn't wait well." He drained the rest of his beer and tossed the can into the open garbage. He walked haltingly over to the refrigerator and deposited the rest of the beer. On the top shelf was a dinner plate covered in foil. "I'll eat that when I get home." He turned, wincing, back to the door. "I'm sorry Jean," he said. He heard her sigh as he walked out into the night air. The bug zapper next door sounded.

. . .

Crate drove over the back roads to Dexter's house for the second time that night. The moon shone round and full in the sky, and all the lights were on in Dexter's house. By the time he'd reached the porch, the lights had gone off, except for the porch. Dexter stepped out to meet him.

"Hey," Crate said.

"I already heard," Dexter said. "That cocksucker Jimmy had me on the phone in minutes. They mess you up bad?"

"I don't know. I got a bad feeling about the ribs, but nothing I can't deal with."

"I got a bigger problem, now," Dexter said. "The fuck did you say?"

"I asked for Jimmy. They sent me to that tattoo parlor. The artist and this Jimmy dude fucked my shit up and took the package."

"Did he say why?" Dexter lit a cigarette, his fingers trembling. Crate could tell now he was out of his mind.

"I guess he didn't like the way I talk," Crate said.

Dexter snorted. "No. I guess not." He blew smoke out his nostrils. "This shit will not flush, Crate."

"I got to get home, Dex. I'll get you some money. To make up for it. It's just going to take some time."

"Naw, naw." Dexter said, flipping his hand. "We're going to have to settle this shit soon."

"How do you mean?"

" I mean we're going to go up there and reason with the motherfuckers." Dexter lifted his shirt and revealed the butt of a handgun.

"Oh no," Crate said. "I can't do shit like that anymore. I got a family."

"I got a girl too. I probably got kids, too, all over this county and the next. They have my money. I don't take it to them, I'm weak. I can't be weak." Dexter fondled the gun.

Crate shook his head. "No. Uh-uh. I have to work tomorrow."

"You can work the whole fucking week, I don't care. We go this weekend."

"Shit, Dex."

"Gird your loins, motherfucker. I told you we weren't playing." Dexter tossed the cigarette butt into a planter, joining a bunch of others. "Go home and get some sleep. I'll text you. on Friday."

"What am I going to tell Jeanelle?"

"Fucked if I know. Tell her the same thing I tell Caitlin. Nothing."

Dexter turned his back and closed the door. The last light in the house winked out, and Crate heard him stumbling around in the dark. Idiot. Off the porch, peepers sounded, and for a moment, Crate remembered being a kid and sleeping out in the yard, hearing the same thing and wondering at what point in the night they'd stop. He tried to stay up all night then to find out but fell asleep, and that was the way he felt right now. His stomach seized. His old life came up in his throat, and he choked it back.

. . .

He took the long way home, and by the time he'd made it back it was nearly 1:00 AM and he had to be at work at 4:00, so he said fuck it. Up all night. Jeanelle had turned off all the lights but the living room and the bare bulb over the door. He clanged the screen door shut and the new puppy nosed at his feet. He let him out briefly to shit before settling down with a single beer and a bottle of water. Turning the TV on, he found some MMA reruns from years past and picked the dog up into his lap. The dog hit his stomach with all four paws and Crate nearly heaved, he was in so much pain.

Crate knew tomorrow would be brutal, beat up and with no sleep, so he took the beer down quickly, then the water. The puppy stuck his nose up for a scratch. What would the weekend bring? He wouldn't feel any better by then, and Dexter would expect him to go in and try to kick these guys asses or worse. It'd be big talk for Dexter, that skinny Shaggy-looking motherfucker, but the real thing for Crate. And there was that big tattoo artist to think about. They couldn't break in there like criminals – don't disrespect the pizza joint – so it was hard to know what exactly Dexter had in mind. They'd have to have a plan, and Dexter didn't plan much, so that left Crate. Planning was not his strong suit.

It made sense to try to hit them at home, rather than the pizza place or the tattoo parlor, but then there'd be wives and kids and girlfriends to think of. The only thing to do, Crate decided, would be to hit them somewhere in between. He took another sip of the water and opened his eyes. Onscreen, the fighters clinched on the cage, the bigger man working inside with wild elbows, and the smaller man took one on the chin and crumpled in place. He closed his eyes again momentarily and felt Jean's weight settle on the cushion next to him.

"I know you don't want to hear this," Jeanelle said.

"Then just don't say it."

"We can figure something out. We can borrow money from Cal."

"Sure. Cal – need to borrow some money. For a drug deal I fucked up. That won't work, Jean."

"He doesn't have to know what it's for."

"He's going to know." Crate's head thumped against the back of the couch. "I'm a fuckup."

"No, you're not," Jeanelle said. "You're a hard-working man who supports his family the right way."

"I used to be."

"Don't let what you used to be fuck up the now. I need you. Jeff needs you. This stupid dog needs you." Jeanelle grabbed his arm. "It's his money. Let him deal."

"He trusted me to do a job. I fucked it up. Now I

need to make it right."

"We will. We'll get the money."

"It's not about the money. Dexter counted on me. I need to fix this."

"For Christ's sake, Creighton. Listen to yourself." Crate stayed silent and let her breath come heavy. She sighed. "I'm going to bed."

Crate took the dog by the scruff and deposited him on the floor. The interviewer on the TV shoved a mic into a bloody fighter's face, who spoke and gestured to the camera with one finger, shaking it. Crate set the alarm on his phone for 4:30 AM. He could get two hours of sleep and push it, still get to work on time.

. . . .

By two in the afternoon, Crate had caught his second wind. He'd been able to skate by the first part of the day breaking rocks and now it was down to learning to operate a loader, which took up time and didn't put much strain on his stomach muscles. He had lots of time to think about how Dexter might handle the situation this weekend. He'd go in balls to the wall, Crate figured, and get them both hurt or killed. He'd have to let Dexter take the lead, but he couldn't let it get out of hand, either. No good, either way. He angled the bucket into a pile of number four gravel and rammed it in, rocks spilling off the side. He dumped the partial and reloaded, as he'd been heavy on the right hand side and got a more balanced load, which he turned and deposited in a waiting dump truck. He had five minutes before another truck showed up, so he set the brake and got out of the loader to piss.

He wondered if Dexter had any notion of bringing someone else in to support them. Dexter, skinny and pale, wasn't exactly intimidating except in his crazy eyes and they'd already beat the shit out of Crate, so it only made sense, but then someone else would know Dexter's business. He'd just have to wait and see how Dexter played it. The rest of the afternoon passed without incident, and he greased the loader, washed up, and left. On the way home, he stopped at a grocery store and bought a bouquet of some flowers for Jeanelle and a stuffed puppy for Jeff. He didn't have to be a fuckup.

When Crate arrived at the trailer, he saw Cal's truck parked next to Jeanelle's. He swore under his breath, reefed himself out of the cab angrily and felt a rib pop. He put a hand on his side before he'd thought about it. Jeanelle had tied the dog to the cinder block steps with a length of chain, and he'd already run a half-circle of grass down to the dirt. He paused with the flowers, and scratched the dog's head, then went inside.

"Hi baby," Jeanelle said, holding out her hands. "They're beautiful. Thank you." Cal sat in the recliner, hands clasped, a sweating can of beer on the table. Crate bent down and gave the stuffed puppy to Jeff, who smelled its head briefly then abandoned it to play with a set of plastic rings.

"So what brings you here, Cal?" Crate said, opening the fridge for his own beer.

"All right. I'll come to the point. Jeanelle says you need money. I'm not going to ask why. She says you need it, and her mother and I are in a position to help. Once. I gave Jeanelle a thousand dollars. Consider it an interest-free loan to be repaid when you can."

"Give him back the money, Jeanelle." Crate cracked open the beer.

"Can I talk to you alone?" Jeanelle said.

"I don't want to get into this," Cal said, standing up. "I'm going to go see your mother."

"Thank you, Cal," Jeanelle said.

"Give him back the fucking money, Jean." Crate said.

"Once," Cal said, and slammed the door behind him.

"Now I owe two people," Crate said. "Fucking great."

"But you can pay off Dexter now."

"That doesn't make me any less a punk," Crate said. "I still have to go see those guys. And now I owe Cal a grand. I'm twice fucked."

"But better to owe Cal than Dexter. You don't have to do anything else illegal."

"Yeah I do."

"Can't you try to give Dexter the money?"

"The money's not the issue. Now Dexter looks weak. Now I look weak. Dexter especially can't afford that, and I'm the one who made him look that way. There's no way this gets better." Crate opened another beer and drained it, then opened another.

Jeanelle looked at him sharply and gathered Jeff

and the diaper bag up in one hand and left.

"Where you going?" Crate yelled after her, but heard nothing but the truck door slam.

. . .

By the time Jeanelle returned Crate had calmed down and stopped drinking, He wanted a clear head for the argument he knew was coming, Jeanelle had turned the truck off and sat in the seat with her head leaned back against the seat, Jeff behind her in the car seat, for a long moment as Crate watched her from the living room window where he'd been anxiously awaiting her.

She banged through the front door and without a word handed him the baby, who gurgled and slapped at Crate, happy to see him. Crate was happy too, as the baby gave him something to concentrate on other than the mess he was in with Dexter and now with Jeanelle. Crate took a sniff and knew the baby needed changing, so he laid him down on the couch and took care of business. By the time he'd finished Jeanelle had come out from the bedroom, the color in her cheeks high. Crate set the baby on the ground, where he immediately toddled over to the dog and started pulling at his ears, which the dog took in good humor.

"So I did it," Jeanelle said, sitting down near Jeff, her hand trailing his hair.

"Did what now?" Crate said, careful with his tone.

"I took the money to Dexter." Jeanelle lit a cigarette from a new pack. He hadn't known her to smoke in the five years they'd been married. She might as well have announced she was from another planet. The news was that bad.

"Why did you do that?" Crate said.

"Because I didn't think you would do it," Jeanelle said.

"I can't do it," Crate yelled. "You might just as well have handed him my balls."

"I did it for Jeff. For us. You don't have to do anything."

"Jesus," Crate said. "You fucked this up good." As if on cue, Crate's phone buzzed. "You know this is Dexter," Crate said. "This ain't ever going to be done now." He looked at the phone. COME OVER, the text read. No hey man. No nothing. Just about what he'd expected.

"He's got his money," Jeanelle said. "Now he needs to leave you alone." On the floor, the puppy yelped and snapped at the baby, and Jeanelle picked Jeff up as he began to howl, more out of surprise than hurt.

"You think this is simple, Jean." He shook the phone at her. "I'm into him now worse than I was."

"No you're not." Jeanelle swayed the baby back and forth on her hip, Jeff sobbing now in hiccups.

"Yes. I am." Crate stuffed the phone into his pocket and picked up his keys, stopping first in the bedroom for his .357, which he shoved into the front of his pants and hung a flannel shirt over it so Jean wouldn't see. "I'm going up there to fix this now," Crate said, slamming the door behind him. Outside, the sun had drawn down into a simmering orange ball, and he headed in its opposite direction. Toward Dexter.

. . .

On the way over, he rehearsed what he would say to Dexter. They needed to hit them tonight. Crate needed to be done with this. They could drive up to the pizza place and reason this out man to man. If it went sour, Crate could scare them with the .357, but he had no intention of shooting anyone or even bringing it out. Having it gave him, not confidence exactly – he knew better than that, from the bad old days – but the knowledge that if he played everything right, he could be out from under this huge thing he'd gotten himself into.

He turned into Dexter's driveway and swore under his breath. Robbie Moore's truck parked next to Dexter's crotch rocket. A bad sign. Crate hoped it washis girlfriend come to visit Dexter's woman, but he knew it wouldn't be. His luck couldn't be that good. Sure enough, as he turned off the ignition, Dexter and Robbie stepped out onto the porch, Robbie in the same stupid cowboy hat he'd worn when fighting Crate over the pup.

"Hello Crate," Dexter said. "Jeanelle already paid me. Kinda surprised to see you."

"Anybody'd send a woman to do his work for him," Robbie began.

"Shut up," Dexter said. "Now what do you want?"

"First off, I didn't send Jeanelle. She got the money and came by herself. I didn't know a thing about it," Crate said. Robbie snorted and Crate turned toward him. "Look. I got something I need to talk with Dexter about. Can you take a hike?" Robbie and Dexter exchanged glances.

"You can talk in front of Robbie. He's my main man," Dexter said. Crate ignored that crack. He'd been under the impression he was Dexter's main man, but then, it seemed as if he might have been played again.

"Fine," Crate said. "I want to hit those guys tonight."

"Jeanelle paid me off," Dexter said. "She led me to understand you were done with me."

"Well, I'm not." His ribs twinged. "Those guys beat the piss out of me. They took the package."

"Jesus Christ, Crate. It wasn't a package. It was pills. Pills I can't sell now, and money I didn't have until your wife gave it to me, no thanks to you, and now I have to deal with people thinking my word is shit. Trust. You can't buy it right now." Dexter spit into the planter.

"Let's go up there tonight when that pizza place closes and hit them."

"And do what exactly?"

"Get my money," Crate said. "They'll have enough deposited to make up for the money Jean gave you. We split the money fifty-fifty. It looked like a busy place, and I know from their website they're cash only and open till one AM. If we hit them about 1:45 we should be fine."

"You want to rob them?"

"Didn't they rob you? Us? Probably broke a rib on me. It's not robbery. They owe me, and we're going to collect." Crate folded his arms.

"You believe this guy?" Dexter said. "This sounds like the old Crate, back when he was a bad old boy."

"I don't trust a man gets his ass kicked twice in a week," Robbie said.

"You didn't kick my ass," Crate said. "I quit. There's a difference."

"How do we know you're not going to quit halfway tonight?" Robbie said.

"So it's we now?" Crate asked. Dexter's silence answered him.

"Three way split," Robbie said.

"Done," Crate said.

"So what do we do until 10 or so?" Robbie said.

"I can think of some things to do," Dexter said. "I got a fistful of Adderall and enough 5.56 to choke a horse. Let's shoot some barrels till dark."

"All right," Robbie said. "I got some roll-up earplugs

in my glove box." Crate simply nodded. The whole night returned him to the man he'd been ten years ago, before Jeanelle, before Jeff, before he'd had a real job and something to lose. It felt bad, honestly, but he knew if they pulled it off, he'd have the money back to repay Cal and then some. Jeanelle's voice came to him then, but he pushed it back in his mind.

. . .

"Pow! I gutted that fucker," Robbie said, bringing the AR-15 down from his shoulder. Sure enough, about thirty yards out, the 55-gallon drum Dexter had filled sloshed water from fifteen holes before Dexter grabbed the rifle from him.

"Watch this," Dexter said, pulling the rifle smoothly up. Bap-bap-bap-bap. The reports echoed down the ridge, and Crate dug the plugs from his ears. In the sudden silence somewhere downhill a dog howled, and the sun was nearly gone.

"We about killed it," Robbie said, tipping his cowboy hat back. "Crate, are you going to take a knock at it?"

"Naw, I'm good." Crate could feel the weight of the .357 dragging the front of his drawers down.

"Suit yourself," Dexter said, his eyes glittering. "Let's go inside and hook up the Playstation. That *Fallout 4* kicks some ass."

"Dogmeat," Robbie said.

"Fucking aye," Dexter said. "That fucker sticks by you. I've never had a dog like him." He thrust the disc into the station.

"That's because most dogs don't care as long as you feed them," Robbie said, jostling the controller up and down in his hand.

"Not right," Crate said. "Dogs love just like people."

"Dogs love like people, he says." Dexter said. "You're the strangest fucker, Crate."

Just then Dexter's girlfriend Caitlin stepped into the room. She came over and sat on Dexter's lap and looked deep into his eyes. "Hooboy. You're wired for sound."

"Damned straight," Dexter said, grabbing her around the waist and pulling her close. "I need a comedown."

"Not with these boys here," Caitlin said. Crate thought of Jeanelle.

"We're going to see a man about a horse," Dexter said, getting up and pulling Caitlin by the hand. "You guys keep yourselves loose." Crate closed his eyes briefly and opened them again to watch Caitlin's ass as she walked into the other room with Dexter and immediately felt guilty

"I'll be damned," Robbie said, his eyes distant. "He's got two characters in here, one named Dexter and one named Fuckhead."

"Play under Fuckhead," Crate suggested. Robbie snorted and started the game.

. . .

About 1:00 AM they'd parked in the adjoining strip mall to Granny's Pizza and the tattoo parlor. Robbie had gone in to the tattoo parlor under pretense of getting a tattoo and reported that the big fucker, Mack, who'd helped beat Crate up, was not in fact working. Instead, he'd found a slim woman with jet-black hair and piercings all up and down her face doing the art. This was a good sign, Crate thought. They pulled masks over their faces and Robbie left his goddamned cowboy hat in the car.

Crate went first, heart in his throat, Dexter and

Robbie close behind. They staked out the back door and hit it when Jimmy came out to empty the fryer grease.

"You don't know what you're doing," Jimmy said. Crate pulled the .357 from his front and heard Dexter mutter under his breath.

"Give us the money, motherfucker," Robbie said, pushing Jimmy in the chest. Crate motioned to Jimmy with the gun, trying his best not to speak and reveal his voice. Jimmy went in and popped the register with a no sale. Crate stuffed the money into a backpack without counting it. "Now the safe," he said in a low rough voice.

"Motherfucker, this ain't all pizza money. You are going to have some serious problems if you fuck me over."

"Just open the safe," Robbie said. Crate poked the man in the head with the .357, cocked it. Jimmy quailed, and on his knees, prodded open the safe with shaky fingers. Crate took all the bills with one hand still holding the gun on Jimmy, large bills first, most of them fixed with rubber bands, but some with the paper bank bands still on them. Dexter flipped his hand in a *come on* motion. Crate handed Robbie the gun then took a roll of duct tape out of the pack and expertly hauled Jimmy's arms behind his back and fixed them with the tape, stuffing an old rag in his mouth and taping it shut. He layered his legs the same way while Dexter and Robbie stood there trembling. He uncocked the weapon and stuffed it back in his pants. They left and slammed the back door shut. All told it had taken maybe fifteen minutes. Jimmy'd get out of the tape, but it would be a while, and by that time they'd be on their way back home, sailing down route 81 with a load of cash.

"God DAMN, Crate. I didn't know you had it in you. That went slick as piss." Dexter held the bag in his hand, counting. They'd tossed the masks in a nearby Dumpster and Robbie had put the goddamned cowboy hat on again. He sat in the back seat jiggling his leg against Crate's seat.

"Would you quit your diddling?" Crate said. "You're killing my back."

"How much?" Robbie said, rubbing his hands together.

"Looks like a little more than $4400," Dexter said. "Hot damn. We're gonna pull this off."

"I swear, Crate. If I'd known –" Robbie began.

"For Christ's sake, Robbie. Shut up." Crate kept his hands on the wheel. "Divide that shit up. Even number of bills each. Rounds out to just under $1500 each. I'm keeping the loose change." Neither of the men argued with him.

"The best part is, they don't even know it was us," Robbie said.

"I wouldn't count on it," Crate said. "I just want you to know. Both of you. If you ever breathe a word about this I'm coming for you. Because I'm never doing this again." Neither man spoke aloud, but Crate caught them exchanging glances. He'd have to deal with them later. He'd dealt with worse inside, though. And suddenly, like a bucket of water dropped on him from above, he was in it. All over again, with so much more to lose. He'd be looking over his shoulder for the rest of his life now. Again.

NOTES

Bad Old Boy originally appeared in *Gollad Review*.
Number A originally appeared in *Beat to a Pulp*.

ABOUT THE AUTHOR

Myron Sherman grew up in the foothills of Appalachia with a horde of dogs and cats. In childhood, a horny stallion bit him in the head as he built a snowman. He lost some skin and hair then but views the world with equanimity now.

MORE PRIMAL POCKET TITLES:

War in the Time of Love · Len Quimby

PRIMAL PUBLISHING
PO Box 1179 · Allston, MA 02134
primal.pub

www.ingramcontent.com/pod-product-compliance
Lightning Source LLC
LaVergne TN
LVHW032014070526
838202LV00059B/6446